What Women Know, What Men Believe

Johns Hopkins: Poetry and Fiction

John T. Irwin, General Editor

WHAT WOMEN KNOW,
WHAT MEN BELIEVE

Wyatt Prunty

THE JOHNS HOPKINS UNIVERSITY PRESS

Baltimore and London

This book has been brought to publication with the generous assistance of the G. Harry Pouder Fund and the Albert Dowling Trust.

The Johns Hopkins University Press,
701 West 40th Street, Baltimore, Maryland 21211
The Johns Hopkins Press Ltd., London

The paper used in this publication meets the minimum requirements of American National Standard for Information Sciences — Permanence of Paper for Printed Library Materials, ANSI Z39.48–1984.

Library of Congress Cataloging-in-Publication Data

Prunty, Wyatt.
   What women know, what men believe.

   (Johns Hopkins, poetry and fiction)
   I. Title. II. Series.
PS3566.R84W46   1986   811'.54   85-24095
ISBN 0-8018-3327-2
ISBN 0-8018-3328-0 (pbk.)

Some poems in this volume appeared, some in slightly different form, in the following periodicals: *Agenda*: "Husband"; *Chowder Review*: "The Field Trip" and "The Mole"; *Gambit*: "From Inside"; *Nebo*: "When Sorry's Not Enough"; *New England Review and Bread Loaf Quarterly*: "The Vireo"; *New Republic*: "The Distance into Place" and "Sleep"; *The New Yorker*: "Black Water"; *Parnassus*: "The Gnostic at the Zoo," "Orpheus," "A Retirement Catalogue," "Wallace Stevens Remembers Halloween," "To Ed, with Alzheimer's," "Getting My Son to Sleep," "Two Kinds of Cause," "Sisters," and "Saying It Back"; *Ploughshares*: "Mother and Spring" and "Our Neighbor"; *Poetry Miscellany*: "The Party"; *Poetry Now*: "The Mole" and "Insomnia"; *Sewanee Review*: "A Winter's Tale," "The Player Piano," and "To My Father"; *Southern Review*: "Geography"; *Tendril*: "Rooms without Walls"; *Verse*: "What Doesn't Go Away." Forthcoming in *New Virginia Review*: "The Depression, the War, and Gypsy Rose Lee."

For Merle and Ian

CONTENTS

A WINTER'S TALE

for Ian

Silent and small in your wet sleep,
You grew to the traveler's tale
We made of you so we could keep
You safe in our vague pastoral,

And silent when the doctors tugged
Heels up your body free of its
Deep habitat, shoulders shrugged
Against the cold air's continent

We made you take for breathing.
Ian, your birth was my close land
Turned green, the stone rolled back for leaving,
My father dead and you returned.

I

Distances

Drawn into what withdraws, drawing toward it and thus pointing into the withdrawal, man first is man. His essential nature lies in being such a pointer.

HEIDEGGER

GEOGRAPHY

The United States is a Cartesian spiral, sweeping away everything and yet boringly level. — ALEXANDER VON HUMBOLDT

Earth writing, like a hieroglyph
That someone scratched in clay before he left
The place he lived, imagined new
And worked to change. Terraced mountains
Rounding like contour lines along a map,
Or homesteads blocked, squared mile on mile,
And green under the surveyor's level:
Immigrants who moved across a continent
Reduplicating roof lines stark
As their abrupt religions,
They wore the land like rivers running,
And those rivers bore the mind's morphology.

If we're still and watch for long enough
The curving back will evidence itself;
The hybrid seed repeat its past
With a small, wild fruit unfit to eat,
Or thoroughbred, all promise when he's born,
Stand dwarfish, a throwback to another time.
We measure what returns with clocks,
Calendars, and genealogies
Never quite accurate because
What we believe is round or straight
Turns out to be as elliptical
As our monkish hope to make things whole.

The means by which one finds his way
Is what he knows, not where he's been
But how he went; the land he reads
Trails in the act of his reading it:
Old barns that let the light break through,
A father with a span of mules for plowing
Who owned a car he couldn't drive,
And windmills overhead that pumped
Aquifers for their slow circularity;
Fixations of happiness, old protections found,
Like daydreams housed by structures
One carries to every place he lives.

Wind moves across wide fields ahead
Of changing weather, cold fronts that make
The trees bend back like weather vanes reversed
Under low clouds. The memory of this
Turns the wind's movement into bent trees,
Activity reduced to one who views,
Like a signature that disappears.
The geographer's space compresses time:
The angular roof stands fixed against
Its local weather, telling us by its pitch
How much snow to expect; the child inside
Will carry that roof through many climates.

One moves to where he finds good work,
Settling there perhaps for life, his children
Grown more a part of where he lives
Than he would ever think to be. For him
After work, the town is mostly dark,
The traffic jugged with stop and go
Jostling as false dichotomies beneath
Clouds blanking stars like the multiples
Of everything he ever wished.
The recognizable green, yellow, and red
Hang overhead in a blowing rain as those
Who drive power by without looking up.

At home, he keeps mementoes framed
On walls paneled with boards he's pulled from barns,
The weathered look his hunger for a past.
On clear nights when he walks out after dinner
The sky rolls its complete stars over
His roof and naked eyes as if
The wind had gotten hold of it.
Along the sidewalk, he stops, head tilted back,
Gazing myopically
Under a concave question raised
Much the way one opens an umbrella
That, caught by the wind, suddenly tugs up.

THE DEPRESSION, THE WAR, AND GYPSY ROSE LEE

H. L. Mencken called me an ecdysiast. I have also been described as deciduous. The French call me a déshabilleuse. In less refined circles I'm known as a strip teaser. — GYPSY ROSE LEE

In a photograph now left to me
Two people lock their arms and pose;
Leaning against a car's black, boxy side,
Cigarettes held out, eyes squinting,
My parents smile into the sun,
So close their white clothes blur
Into one image.
                    It's 1938;
Most things are cheap and unaffordable,
The war ahead with money to spend
And nothing to buy, ready as any

                                        substitute
To draft people from part-time jobs
To a full-time hitch,
                            and anonymous
As orders through the mail,
                                    or targets
That synchronize with calendars
And newsreels ticking black and white.

Soon things will be standardized,
The prefab buildings, starched uniforms,
Haircuts, and requisitioned tires,
Even the Big Band Sound on radios
Whose dials illuminate the stilled faces
Of those listening for news between
Two coasts darkened against attack.

Traveling west at forty-five,
My parents will drive at night to duck the heat
And save the rationed, recapped tires
That peel their tread regardless what.

Promises.
                All California long.
Belief, an exhausted Chevrolet
With running boards and rings gone bad,
They call it Gypsy Rose Lee because
It's only got the bare essentials . . .
But takes them out answering orders
By traveling nights and sleeping days,
Helps detour them through one dull rental
After another for five years.

Later, an academic life.
They lose one child, have three more,

                                progress,
Until the body's fractions add up
Against its certainties.
                         Sometimes
A radio left on all night
Because the weather's hot and still;
No one can sleep, but no one talks
Either.
         Or a dog barks at a car
Passing too slowly to be going
Anywhere but home, so late
That being late doesn't matter anymore.

Sometimes necessity becomes its own
Dwindling fact, like the stripper's need
For money,
               whose name they gave their car,
A joke to reconcile them to the things
They wanted then but couldn't have,
Like Kilroy, who only wanted to go home;

And beyond necessity, some hope
For other things put in the names
They gave to their children, to each other,
And the explanations handed their children
Because explaining things becomes
A way of naming them also.

Locked arms to pose a photograph
Surviving all these two survived,
No hint of what they saw ahead
Making them smile
                    except
The camera's implicit place,
Circular and reflecting
Out of its own dark precision,
Dark like the theaters where people sat
Taking in short, censured newsreels
And narrow as the wised-up cold war
That followed,
                    shadowing
The corny jokes on television,
Canned laughter over whiz-bombs, trick ties
With lights blinking across the *fifties*,
One whoopee-cushioned sigh of relief . . .

Like the relief reckoned by Gypsy Rose Lee
Writing her memoirs in 1955,
Addressing them to her son
And counting everything she owned,
Enumerating respectability,
The Rolls with matching luggage, the house
In New York on East Sixty-third
Complete with pool and elevator —
"Some little things removed,
Some big ones gathered up."

One innocence erodes another,
With neither one accurate in what
It pushes forward like a handbill
Or cart loaded with incidentals;
And no one cautions against the little things
Adding up in closets and storage rooms
To another set of incidentals,
Building toward one solemn rummage sale
Held, after the last big fire and funeral,
In everybody's yard,
                              but casual now
As a part-time worker taking orders
Or soldier on temporary duty,
Casual as someone sick
Who is left alone, dozing among
The pastel cards well-wishers have sent . . .

A several and sad innocence,
That spot an audience will watch
When a magic trick takes place,
Distraction made unique yet shared
And similar to the way you tighten
Inwardly to smile or seem natural
When someone takes your picture,
                              the day
Brought down to one approximation,
Leaving each one a little foolish,
Like a naked man whose navel's full of lint.

But in this photograph that's left
To me it's 1938.
                              Everything is
Ahead like something on a map
That someone reads in a car at night,
The road jostling a flashlight so
The map is hard to figure out,
This picture that they leave,
                              the one I find

Which now becomes a photograph I take
Of someone photographing me.
Cameras zoomed into each other,
Two lenses fix on interiors
That stop down to blank shutters cutting
Part to smaller part, like mirrors set
In a barber shop, facing
Their diminishing reflections.

Even diminishment provides
A kind of movement,
                              an always falling,
Like motion sickness,
                              but felt the way
An overloaded plane lifts off
Then doesn't climb but runs for miles
Barely above the trees until
Gathering speed
                     the nose tilts up
And looking back you feel yourself
Dropping away
                     through what you see.

THE DISTANCE INTO PLACE

Dolls in gallery along her walls,
she'd broken one so, bending down,
opened a sewing box then knelt,
the needle's eye narrowing her gaze
to fractions in a room where clothes
and broken doll cluttered the floor.

Forty-three and already gray,
she focused on a wilderness
of close particulars, a bird
imagining a cage, her eyes
turned like an animal's caught by
a car's headlights, reflecting blind
and lost inside the light they saw.
Later, the family away at church,
she used a butcher knife to carve
initials in the dining room table.

On Sundays, we drove to Memphis
where each visit I waited in the car,
studying the windows I was told
were hers, my talented aunt,
playing the piano as soon as she
could stand, homely, proud, and silent.
No photograph could get a smile.
The term I heard was that she was
afflicted.
                My parents spoke in fragments
as riding home I strained to catch
a phrase that held the syntax to her name.
Those trips, made thirty years ago,
we stepped out of our upright cars,
mother and grandmother in hats and gloves,
my father smoking, fedora cocked
ironically but eyes measuring
the distance out ahead as though
he walked into some fixed perspective.

Cold nights the house contracts
to the tightness of its carpenter's
precise intent, leveled and squared
again as if to match his mind.
A car's headlights scroll across the wall
as a figure deepens where curtains bell.
It bends and waves, ushering me
beyond the place it disappears
dark into dark and soft, a thing
coagulate as guilt in memory,
as my aunt, childishly petulant yet old
and fluttering like an antique doll,
a miniature of iced velocities.

Broad day, I kneel to gather scrub
grown up along the barbed-wire fence
that frames our farm. The fields
are frozen hard, resistant as
the locust posts punctuating each fence.
The stream is skimmed with ice and makes
a fixed division of the land.
But night, when I wake to a figure
idling across my wall, dissolving
dark, the surface of that stream
cuts to a slower, colder path.

One name becomes the secret to another,
blue into gray, like rain, and gray
to deeper blue, till all the down-rush
we anticipate, the waking sleep of things,
turns to a clarity like pain.
I see my aunt, alone and still,
her room cluttered with the objects of
intentions neither she nor her doctors knew
because mutation made its own way
through her life, carving its initials
as the code that waits inside a seed,
its rope-like strands curling into thought,
and that thought in turn a distance we contrive.

ROOMS WITHOUT WALLS

Late sunlight breaking through the room
And a boy's round face against the glass,
Breath clouding, eyes narrowed to the sun.
Outside, snow falls through the light;
The sky is granular and close,
All pattern of the wind's white slant,
That wind about the house, and branches'
Snow-muffled scrapes against the eaves.

Later, the power lines will fail,
And, twelve years old, I will stand outside
Counting the coal oil lamps that float
From room to room as though our house
Did not have walls inside but was
One space through which my family sent
Their liquid light without effort,
Like quiet conversation.

All this before the heart disease,
Cancers, and little suicides
Of cigarettes and whiskey turned
Events into a daguerreotype
Fading and slightly out of focus.
The snow, deeper than ever before,
Was in a frame I took outside
But never brought back in again.

Instead, with power lines knocked down
All over town, I stamped in the street,
My feet so cold they hurt, and gazed
Until I turned my family's warm house
Inside out, the snow's unfolding linen
And pillows deep as a child's gathering
Unconsciousness that sleeps through any sound
Made for the mind's stark furnishings.

Two blocks past where I stood, small shacks began,
Unpainted shotguns shouldered together
Into a row of narrow facings
I studied from the school bus window
Or counted as our car drove past —
Ten to a block, identical,
Each with its small front yard
Of bright red clay, as hard as pavement.

From that direction, over the stillness
The snow had brought, I heard the blows
And the high voice of a small girl
Who could not beg but only gasp
"Daddy, Daddy" between the cracking sounds
Made by whatever he'd picked up.
I stood more still than I had ever thought.
He beat her until there was silence.

And I think that action took forever.
More than the snow's cold multiplicity
Or all the lights that failed to work
In our small town, or hands that rested
In laps, in pockets, near telephones,
The hands of those who waited for
The power, thinking the novelty
Of such a deep snow, and that far south.

And later that night, beyond crying,
I began to shake for that small child,
For both of us; not in the arms and legs
But in the chest and gut. And I felt
As though I had a fishing line
In my head, drawn to the point of breaking.
And when I closed my eyes a light
Would flash, then run like iodine.

What I know now is that the frame
Made by the window where I stood
One afternoon was cold and arbitrary.
If anything, the snow's white sifting
Down my glass meant anonymity
Far past the best or worst we ever do,
Beyond all melting at our touch
Which like regret arrives past tense.

What I know is that our meanings work
Like games thought up by children in a street;
The space, number of players, goals
And objects moved are arbitrary.
And yet our games are serious,
As players go beyond themselves
Into a violence that wins,
And lets us say they were responsible.

The house I saw outside that night
Was covered by a heavy snow
That rounded all its borders; no hedge
Or wall could separate its space
From a smaller space two blocks away,
The place of one small girl's great pain,
Which still echoes in the stillness that we are.

II

Thin Gravities

What we encounter at first is never what is near, but always only what is common. It possesses the unearthly power to break us of the habit of abiding in what is essential, often so definitively that we never come to abide anywhere.

HEIDEGGER

BLACK WATER

A fly on black water stands
Over himself on stilts, the poise
Of his slick reflection bobbing
Between water and eye, two mirrors
Facing an infinite digression.

How does the image he sees
Diverge into the things we name,
Eyes, thorax, spiracles? He strides
Water stilled under maples mixing light
Until one sees no separate thing.

All day trout glide silently beneath color
And reflected color where margins fail.
They swim with the heart's determined monotone,
Hungry for our imagist, who hovers
Light as the maple's paired wings and seeds.

THE GNOSTIC AT THE ZOO

Man is the as yet undetermined animal. — NIETZSCHE

Fat and bored, pedestrian
Behind their bars, they do not bear
The riddle that we bring
Like a twisted spine or guttural
Expressing pain before pain is felt.
Instead, they sleep and loaf beside
their food, casual among the flies
and visitors circling them.

Cage after cage, we round corners
With soft-eyed generalities,
Puttering through catalogues of names,
But feel the harsh comparison
In the eyes of animals fed here
Reflecting like an old analogy.
Then beyond the elephants and giraffes
Exotic birds start chattering
As a young teacher leads her class
Of fourth graders past the cages,
Lecturing on Darwin and Lyell.

Eclectus Parrot, Paradise Whydah,
Purple Throated Euphonia . . .
Distinctions like the fretwork light
The parrots' cage extends across
The children's path mix in the shade
Of finger ferns hung overhead
Softening the heat and humidity
Of a summer afternoon into
The first savannah ever occupied.

They walk, then pause, then walk again,
Ignoring a polar bear's depressed
Indifference, the alligator's
Cold-blooded stare, then,
                      slowing,
Stop to study a half-grown chimpanzee
Hiding behind a tree, where,
In the mute extension of their seeing,
The green shade only moves one way.

THE FIELD TRIP

Believing what the mind contained
the landscape bore as evidence,
our myth was measurement.
We drove miles then hiked to see
the exposed fault our map announced,
wondering if what we had found
was only an analogy,
that our reciprocity with earth
is like a manic conversation,
occurring in an empty room.

On foot, we rose and fell,
looking down more than up,
until we climbed into our car
and powered away quietly.
Then the landscape was a sidelong glance
turned pictograph, the trip's long bidding
arguing us out then home again
where we thought our day into distance.

From where to everywhere in one day
is a nice trick, the car's shadow
along the road a dark, confident wing
covering its presupposed way.
Under the sky's blue commonplace
we gaze as far as we want to,
at the sun cut by a low hill's arch,
or the land rounding its humble place.

HOMESICKNESS

What is it lost by one who leaves
home willingly? His wife is asleep
or tired over coffee, while he looks
toward sunset, sunrise, panoramic scenes
through tinted glass, the coach seat's
somatic bliss almost buoyant
and yet the farther away he goes
the tighter things draw around him.

Dirigible in coat and tie,
he rises to his aisle, then shoulders
among passengers whose faces give
novel angles, mute epigrams
for postcards in the future tense;
sometimes a conversation over drinks
made candid by the fact those speaking
know they will never meet again.

And then he buys a ticket home,
returns and sleeps more heavily
than he has done for weeks. Next day,
his wife's appliances hum dutifully,
as she recalls her father's silence,
her stomach tightening on Sundays
when his bags appeared beside the door.
Her kitchen crowds behind her as she breathes
into the window plants above her sink,
gazes outside, eyes tunneling into
the bruised asphalt turned slick with rain.

ORPHEUS

He gnaws an emptiness
That silences inside itself,
Each backward glance the crooked neck
Of one stiffened by what was lost
When sound had brought her from beneath
And he, in light now, turned too soon,
A moment when conviction fell
Into its own, cold opposite,
A sorrow that made sorrow come.

His turning was that slant felt when
Light angles through an opened door,
The room inside suddenly visible
But no one there, a space that lengthens
Sight, and separates,
                                    till viewed out of
The corner of that room, formally
Yet crooked as any backward path he takes,
He gazes from one, fixed angle toward
Each bright new room he will occupy.

There too light lengthens; and he fails
As habitant. Rooms parallel
Beyond distinction, until he says
"One house."
                    Wide affirmations wait.
They press from underneath so that
He thinks the poverty of light
Seen through a stream's stirred sediment,
Light, land, and water over land
Where lines of sight reflect themselves.
No genesis is adequate.
A revenant with appetite?
A name he says repeatedly.

LIVING ALONE

More avenues than she can follow
beyond brief speculations made
the way a game is played,
                              each street
becomes a backward choice arrived at from
some future need.
                      The traffic shoulders
into one long reboant chorus
bounced between apartment buildings
while from the hall and adjacent rooms
she hears her neighbors coming home,
doors slammed on tattling fragments
as she rounds back,
                          tangential now,
feeling the need for an older landscape
in which she judges distances between
small, scattered houses built along
a railroad track that either way she looks
will place her as it parallels from sight.

The weakening light dissolves her room
into a motion of cars beneath,
while beside her plants and calendar
a picture curls under its glass,
obliquely framing another thing,
the half-light greening astray
among gradual growth.
                    It bends
her shadow past the place she stands
waving to a man whose back is turned,
a broken stretch of trees seen where
two tracks narrow but never touch.

A RETIREMENT CATALOGUE

Brass telescopes with Halley on
The other end, chronometers
Inside their clear acrylic domes,
Tide charts, bird charts, thermometers,
A pendulum of solid chrome . . .
Items meant for a glass-topped desk
Or study window, the polished means
For measurement, a weather check
Without the weather, and time gleaned
By someone running out of time.

This catalogue was mailed to me
"Or Current Resident," in line
For leaving the line, my chance to see
How the list goes on into millions
And we barely stammer, distracted
By our small equipage, gadgets drawn
Ahead as if we had contracted
To make the count,
                              as setting out
Past where the roving jays will rout
And the windchimes clank without relief
The last page turns, the birds cry thief.

THE PLAYER PIANO

Learning from a player piano,
I let my fingers rest on the keys
Until they drop from beneath into sound;
Inside, the mechanical works, set, greased,
And churning ahead of thought, possess
The future tense their builder meant
For the wires he chose, whose vertical stress
Tuned his wood, felt, and cogwheeled instrument.

A continuum of moving parts,
Music made without the variance
Of a slow hand or a false start,
How better to work one's will against chance,
Avoid the twelve-year-old who wrecks the scales,
Silence the adult whistling the *Vogelquartett*?
A century later, my fingers trail
Thought made mechanical, not grand but upright.

THE PARTY

I follow everything I hear,
first down the hall
and then into a closet where,
locking myself, I listen to
our neighbors collected happily,
talking about bermuda grass and lime,
the lack of rain, or too much rain,
till someone stands to tell a joke . . .

then laughter
           like thin plastic cracked
and ice, glasses, and creaking chairs,
and I hunch in the dark behind
my overcoat,
           seeing our smiling neighbors set
their teeth against clear glass, clear ice.

Crazier than all of them . . .
I've never left the room, instead,
forgot to make a drink. Reminded,
I give an addlepated smile
and start across the floor, nodding
to my many likenesses, all button-down,
with tweeds and ties.
           We talk in eddies —
someone holds a brush pressed
to a turning record so it plays
all of the melodies at once,
or, sinking to another density,
the record slows, and each sound divides
into a thread pulled toward its breaking.

Outside, thin branches click against
themselves;
                    encyclopedic pines collect
to a green baize behind which someone
plays with dice.
                    At dusk, the wind starts up
as we, caught in a local idiom,
                    must move about inside,
all smiles and laughter over narratives
that always turn to someone absent.

Choreograph the distances
our voices make,
                    like music terracing
back out across the yard
                              into the trees.

                    We are water pouring into water,
a sound that gathers like the row of pines
outside
          whose branches darken now
just where the sun has flowered down
into
          thin gravities
that lift and lean as the wind kicks up.

FROM INSIDE

I am an ophthalmologist,
my office only a step around
the corner. Also I am
a boxing fan, although
I get to fights less often now.
Sometimes I think I recognize
the stance, but there's no way to ask;
there's more distance than his counter's width,
and talking after I've picked a paper
only gets me change, thrust a little hard.

He is at once an aging rock star
of television and radio
and fat man on a local street
wearing a parrot shirt and fez,
bobbing to music from a tape,
selling magazines and papers to me.
The photographs behind him state
he once possessed an adolescent's
taut washboard belly; glossies
of a young middleweight, gloves up
in peekaboo, all frames identical.

After my stopping here for months,
we still acknowledge nothing.
That is why I was thinking of
walking a different way and buying
from the newsstand in my building,
even today as I arrived and again
tried to say something. I got a look.

His eyes are off a bit, and I
could do a squint for him, no charge.
Shorten one muscle, alignment restored.
It's nothing, just mechanical.
But it was not the sort of look
one likes to get. There's something wrong,
I'm certain something is wrong.
He isn't punch drunk or partly blind,
like some fighters who hold on too long,
but once he looks his gaze won't move.

One remembers how he was seen.
I know the hooded looks
that salesmen like to greet one with.
Also, glazed eyes reversed upon themselves,
speculative yet self-absorbed,
stiff personalities the will
has put into a frame,
celebrities, for example.
Fictive and still. Beneath their eyes,
the camera fixes flesh-torn smiles.
But the moment this man gazed
was different; it made me think
of a large wood moth that struck
a window pane repeatedly,
beating itself against the glass
it could not see. Only the light
mattered. Inside, the glass was dark
where he struggled in my reflection.

WALLACE STEVENS
REMEMBERS HALLOWEEN

for Bill Clarkson

The thing I loved was Halloween.
The children dressed in more colors
than I could count, their multiples
pressed in regiment, wedged and wiggling,
masked giggles in the door's dark frame.
We'd have them in for cider, and,
wearing my tuxedo, I'd bring the cups,
all stiff formality, but watching them
lifting their masks to drink, catching their eyes.

Then off they'd go, their voices all
one high cacophony caroling
into echoes, clamorous groups
with rumpled bags, each thrilled with his own
anonymity on a night once meant
to celebrate the dead.
                              There are no dead,
only the missing, and windows filled
with hollowed fruit and fire inside
lighting our interrupted sleep
much as comedians light laughter
from an audience's partial fears.

But those children made me glad.
I never thought behind the plastic grins
there were smiles waiting expectantly
for a hundred different futures,
for Halloweens no one could calendar.
I never took their peacock dress
and blackbird frequency as randomness,
as anything other than good fun
by miniature Taft Republicans.
They were my winter warblers, siskins
and kinglets, come to the comic feeder.

MISS AMERICA

It's katzenjammer, and she knows it
When the air takes on a density
Shouldering in as clouds contract;
The airport's sock points absolutely down
And pilots' beacon circles back
Against all reckonings.

Opening a tinted door, she meets herself
Reflected where the glass angles inside,
And she looks into a momentary past
Projected through the airport lobby;
Small congregations herd themselves
From elevators, their voices breaking up
Like water over rocks, or rain
Guttering in several directions.

Then someone shouts her name,
A flash goes off,
                              and her arms are lazy tongs,
All waving back and jotting autographs,
Each flash leaving her stunned eyes on
Some middle ground where colors run
The way the sky and water mix
When, swimming, she rolls head back
And does her comic catalina.

But here she moves like smothering down,
Midair and drifting seesaw through
This lobby where the lights go off
Too fast for a confidential wink.
Faces, arms, legs, the graveling crowd.
They are not what she wanted them to be,
And even as her smile fixes,
She is not what they remember.

III

Mother West Wind, Mother Earth

It so happens that he does not have four shillings to his name, and yet he firmly believes that his wife has this delectable meal waiting for him. If she has, to see him eat would be the envy of the elite and an inspiration to the common man, for his appetite is keener than Esau's. His wife does not have it — curiously enough, he is just the same.

KIERKEGAARD

The mere cry dies away and collapses. It can offer no lasting abode to either pain or joy. The call, by contrast, is a reaching, even if it is neither heard nor answered. Calling offers an abode.

HEIDEGGER

FIREFLIES

for Heather

Too many for a child who stumbles
after, steadying her opened jar
to catch, arm's length, a thing
that darkens, moves, then lights again
the way at night an airplane banks
over a city's lights and I
look down wondering what leads me home
past multiples of home.

Suddenly my daughter shouts
she's caught one which, set beside
her bed, will alternate between
the soft green light that leads
its sex ahead and another thing
already cold inside each pause,
till in her sleep the idea of
such light falls through a darkening
that, singled out inside her jar,
will burn until it dies.

THE VIREO

Finding the egg along our drive,
Shell broken but heart still going,
She placed it under the rhododendron,
Hoping the mother might pluck it back alive.

Later, having left it for a while,
She went back and found the small thing
Still moving, having broken a new hole
Where the frail head could be seen thrusting:

Ants, arriving in column,
Had already set about their job.
Child on the way, her voice had a tone
That made me stop at what she described,

The bird turning in its shell
And she having turned it to the ants.
I watched her standing in the hall
Handling the egg as though some want

Had gotten hold of her so close
She hadn't found a name for it,
Much like one turned back to that place
The mind first thinks itself and splits.

That night, unable to sleep, I found myself
Thinking we're not such special animals
But part of all the interrupted lives,
The stuck exits, sudden arrivals,

All of us making them all,
And one small bit of living here in pain
Before it had the chance to clear its shell
And join our predatory chain.

WAITING FOR OUR SECOND CHILD

Out back, leaves spiral
In a northwest wind,
                climbing our ridge
Not in fall's various colors
But February's factual brown.
Settled on the ground three months
And now swept up among limbs,
They drive against our house,
                    while sheltered,
The front yard stands impassively green,
All cedar, laurel, and rhododendron.

Soon you will be tugged from your sleep,
A cesarean child, breathless
But spared contractions and bruising bones.
Until that time, we wait inside
Between two weathers guessing your sex,
Whose eyes, whose nose, what color hair . . .
At once whole and different, spun
Like the oak, maple, and locust leaves
That circle and taxi into our yard;
Rising, darkening, they drop from sight
Then lift again, repeating themselves.
Today those leaves,
                blown in their dry mania,
All look the same, just as the front yard stills,
Featureless in its green acclamation.

THE MOLE

Yesterday he tunneled his way
across our yard, then overnight
reversed himself and, working back
the way he came, made a loop
that closed where he began;
at that point, our neighbor's dog
stopped circling and dug him up.

I found him, practical claws relaxed
and mouth ajar like a subdued chorister,
and remembered a story about moles,
how as a girl my mother had a dog
that dug them up, and a man working the farm
who made fur coats of them for her dolls.

Now, a steady rain settles
our mole's tunneling, and, windows closed,
we listen to the downspout's muffled force,
the wet ground soft as a dog's muzzle;
and our newborn son cries, his voice
like a doll's with its head tipped back.

Rain, and sleep like rain, our blanket settles
into a soggy field on which we stretch
feeling the mud's suction tug us down
into the tightening loop
of an animal trapped because
he turned instinctively,
the mind's tunneling fear above which
it tips head back but cannot cry.

WHEN SORRY'S NOT ENOUGH

When sorry's not enough, we walk away.
Trees darken where we stop; the birds grow still.
We are the weather, cold and gray;
Our barometric children crowd with chills.
Whatever flies is dragged out of the sky;
The birds are small and settled in their guilt.
And reason is a self-sustaining cry
That names the things we own that it has built,
Naming till we cannot name ourselves,
Even follow what the childrens' stories tell —

No limit like a charm that ends by twelve,
No wolf outside, or oven fired like hell
Where birds have eaten the bread-crumb trail
That led from one world into another.
Instead, a sort of joke made of a tale
In which no lesson's taught and no one bothers
To make an end or tell us why
Things work that way, our disappointing acts
Become themselves the end, in which one cries,
Another makes a point, giving the facts.

TO MY FATHER

No cartography could get you here,
No bread crumbs get you back; the forest greens
Beyond distinction, and you feel it grow
Inside like all the landscapes you have seen.

This fall those landscapes color change,
Reminding us the calendar
We reinvent each year is wrong
For its arithmetic. You stare

Through your window, static as a photograph
Focused past its bottled time;
I badger you to fight as if
Your pulse hammered and waltzed again into mine.

The doctors say you are climbing stairs
And out of breath, as they feel your side,
Take X-rays, order respirators,
And leave no place for you to hide,

And yet a way out, another season.
Father, the grammar of disease is change;
Breathe deeply, drink lots of water, use reason
When you can for what you rearrange.

WHAT DOESN'T GO AWAY

His heart was like a butterfly
dropped through a vacuum tube,
no air to lift it up again;
each time the fluttering began,
he opened his eyes, first seeing
his family staggered around the bed,
then seeing that he didn't see.
While he died, the nurses wouldn't budge,
blood pressure gone too low, they said.

I, who used to play bad jokes on him,
my laughter in his shaking head,
bent and held his hand and talked *Lamaze*,
"your breathing, concentrate on your breathing."
And he did, like a well coached athlete,
believing I could get him through
his heart's slow, syncopated pains.
I do not know how long we worked that way,
but after he died I couldn't straighten up.

"Your breathing, concentrate on your breathing,"
instead of, "I love you. Thank you."
A respirator tube put down his throat
made what I'd said to him ridiculous.
One last practical joke, an off-speed pitch
I'll never retrieve.

HUSBAND

Grief is this quiet room we shared,
Your heavy sleep my comfort even when
I lay awake because of you
And waited for the clock to close
My questioning that as a night light
Had the outline of our room but not its feel.
I waited till the birds outside
Began their widening paths for food
Then rose to make your breakfast,
A commonplace ignored yet needed.

Now the house will be too quiet,
Its rooms more spacious than before,
Evading my grasp like the shafts
Of light that skew this waking here alone.
I miss nothing you could give me
But your taking what I gave.

MOTHER AND SPRING

Like our children after Halloween,
we count the keep, rustling bags,
thrilled with our own mild terrors —
the immediate man threading blacktop
or the wind's cold breath around the house.
With spring, birds migrate here to nest,
and we feed them for the need we have
that they come back year after year,
each bird a species returning home.

This year spring came before we thought,
finding you wooden with your daughter's death,
confronting every incident
with a child's irrational fear
of the dark, the stern fragility
of a child shaken by a dream.
No name can seal your loss.
                              For you,
the species is your daughter's face.
Saying child, only the mother is called.

OUR NEIGHBOR

In the kitchen the toaster pops
too quickly, the water boils away
and something burns,
                              and she turns on herself,
a predator breaking a mirror.
Door bell jammed with no one there,
the screen door sags, its rusted mesh
reducing her porch light to squares.

People gather and huddle for advice,
then telephone. Inside, she's crouched
under a table, counting the kitchen tiles
in a voice old as nightmares —
old as her anxious eyes waiting
while sirens multiply the dark
quadrants arcing beyond her porch.

Permanent and printed dress
like hothouse plants she's left untended,
someone leads our limp neighbor to a car.
The flashing lights are quantities cut loose,
serials along our darkened wall,
as new to this neighborhood
and reduced, we sit quietly
in the sum of her departure.

TO ED, WITH ALZHEIMER'S

The little comedies came first,
The car keys lost, your way forgotten,
Names transposed on a floating list
Of friends who never coalesced.

Then the ocean turned your stare to miles,
Gray weather where your people slept
More heavily than before, flexed smiles
Buoying their faces when they met.

Today, your aviary eyes sweep over
Surfaces never touched; the future tense,
Suspended like a child's balloon, hovers
In your quiet room as a paid expense.

You have set your general grin
Against our noise, each thing its type,
And now we follow your thin
Transpositions,
                          the fragile traps
You place to catch our names,
                                              like bells
Marking the waves of voices in a room
With bad acoustics.

INSOMNIA

Count the number of times boards crack
In the cooling house, or furniture plays
Like a thin percussionist tapping his way,
Working the bones over and back,
A blindman's stick or erratic clock,
The door that clicks in its frame as a key
Which someone works in your lock
Without forcing it, works patiently.

SLEEP

Another nomenclature.
Rolling downhill, arms overhead,
my words urging a different voice,
and foreknowledge,
                    sometimes dread,
like Cassandra watching fire;
sometimes lost in a corridor
and profoundly sad at the emptiness,
other moments, blind in that hall
but certain of its end, toward which I walk.

Not just neurons shocked into motion,
but the hidden fear of a buried loss
mapped with a compass whose valence
is desire;
              we want what we already know —
the blueprints to a house and children
filling each room before it is built,
all sorts of structures, a close geometry,
tugged like film across one's forehead.

Some nights, my crying child who really cries.
That's easy. Rise, turn on the light and speak;
at least I answer one set of fears.
Worst, my father calling me for help,
his voice loud as the one he used to call
me home for supper, and locked at a distance.
Sleep, an oblique record of expense,
more than a collage of shapes, sounds, and colors
because our careful covers make it so.

GETTING MY SON TO SLEEP

Crying because kept up too late
He can't give in and go to sleep
But stands up in his crib and tells me
"No, no, light on," refusing to lie
Under the covers I turn for him —
He's learned just how alone he is
When his eyes close and nothing steadies
His falling beyond the place he lies.

Sometimes I rock him, native humming
A soft calypso, hoping he will
Forget his stubbornness and drift
Into the rocker's monotony
As someone on a raft will drift,
At first the waves uncomfortable
But then the sun's persistence lowering
His gaze to the water's curved horizon.

But whether rocked or left to cry,
The covers that I turn against
The fear that makes him call for light
Can't answer what he's learned of sleep,
His falling past a blank horizon,
An opening through which he dives
Breathing his own damp life
Back down to where he drowns toward sleep.

TWO KINDS OF CAUSE

for Barbara

Heaviest snow in years,
I drove at walking speed, my lights
given back to me in thousands
of particles, at once crystalline
and white and falling in a density
that blocked all but the wipers lazing
across the glass
                                till home
I drifted right, bumped the curb and stopped;
then picked a path along our drive
noting the way each window's light
worked differently across the snow,
rectangular blues, purples, and yellows,
the landscape of a children's book
with pastel generalities
rounding a world as soft as it was cold.

Later, walking outside again,
the snow had turned to freezing rain
ticking into its own slick crust;
then later still, another snow,
granular down through the window's light,
like white cells through an artery,
leukemic in their mass and gathering.
I watched the trees and hedges bulge
into a swollen weight that cracked
from branch to trunk to ground
till something snapped, like burning grease
or static. Ten feet away three wires
snaked backwards, igniting where they touched.

Stepping away, I remembered what
I saw one night while walking home
with my father. An ambulance
skidded into a pole and brought
high-tension lines down on its top.
Inside, the black driver was unhurt
but completely still, touching nothing;
the white man in back was dead but near
the lines and partly out a window.
The current made his body jump.
A man behind us laughed at this.
Another teased the driver, who sat
expressionless, eyes straight ahead.

My father's hands were steering me
by the shoulders; we threaded through
the crowd, my head angled toward the wreck
until we turned the corner to our street.
Once home, he used the telephone
then carried me up to bed
only to take a chair and talk
long after I should have been asleep.
When I spoke, my voice was dry and thin;
his talking worked its way around
that change, floating a lower sound
insistent and continuous,
until beyond my questioning I slept.

What happened years ago came back
to me like something handed down.
From the snow-stilled street I turned and saw
our house, first dark then one room with a light,
then flashlights splashing down the hall,
our children giddy in the dark.
Their lights bobbed then stilled beside the door,
floating like the voice that once explained
downed wires, wrecks, the cruelty of jokes,
the way things work when they don't work,
that voice building a screen that sieved
one sort of light and let me sleep.

The snow continued. I worked my way
back to the house. The heat was out.
I built a fire and gathered blankets,
thinking, first named by one then many,
we live out of two kinds of cause —
the snow collecting water for spring,
all colors held yet blank as bone,
the spectrum drawn back into white.

FLORENCE

The weather hot, you held ice
to your neck and wrists;
                          widowed early,
no children, you knew what waiting meant,
and stilled like attic heat
before launching another story.

But not always so still.
                          Your house old,
upstairs its empty bedrooms held
their own set of stories, sister
and mother living there for years,
the children's things your sister kept,
your husband and his brother bankrupt
in twenty-nine . . .
                          your mother's quips
delivered from the second landing hit
their target every time.
                          Then mother gone
and sister committed to a home.
Little of this known by anyone,
and nothing seen in what was done.

Your humor made us comfortable inside
high-ceilinged rooms where stories led
one to another.
                    On trips you sat
up straight, hat secure, and told us what
each curve would bring, five hundred miles
of this on two-lane roads, and smiles
at rationed, wartime tires gone flat,
jack out, my father mad,
                              then laughter
over the peacock feather to your hat
affirming itself in the rearview mirror.

SISTERS

For you see they were to play in the Green Meadows all day long until Old Mother West Wind should come back at night.

They are walking home in tight bunches,
Passing the football field where their brothers
Duck into helmets, like young goats who lunge
Head on. A whistle arcs and no one bothers
To check the time.
                              Then they are dressed
For a party that marks the end
Of a school year *everybody* passed . . .
Bright crinolined dresses casually flattened
Like wafers as they brush through doors
Opening to the stale gymnasium
Where their fathers chaperon a floor
That vibrates like a room-sized drum.

Escaping outside, they are children
Waiting for something they have never seen,
The moon flooding clouds that separate
Into brief, staggered patterns,
Prepotent figures in an old dance
Or young boys touching consequence,
The disparities of loss and birth,
Mother West Wind, Mother Earth.

SAYING IT BACK

One afternoon you step outside
to get the mail and see your son
walking home, looking over his shoulder,
calling to a friend who walks the other way.
And you double back into that time
when Mr. Ryland took you hunting,
age twelve, because once years ago
your grandfather had done the same for him;
and he cautioned you to look back every
fifty steps, "to learn the woods past tense,"
he said. And so you walked ahead,
gun barrel down and turning to look.
Later, game pouches stuffed with quail,
he let you lead the way across the field
into the woods, and then into
all the backward glances you had made,
the trees dividing and birds scolding.

What is the lore to looking back like that?
Your son has barely moved from where
you saw him stepping off the bus.
First sight of him, his turning to call,
and you were twenty years away, at home
in Tennessee with Porter Ryland's father
telling you how your grandfather
could drop four quail with just three shots;
telling you, the best way he knew how,
what to do when the covey flushed
behind you; telling you who you were,
till you had said your way back through the woods.